ENCYCLOPEDIA BROWN looked like the usual ten-year-old boy. Actually he was very *un*-usual. Encyclopedia was a boy who really *used* his eyes and his ears and his head—and his head was full of facts. As for Idaville, where he lived, no grownup, boy, or girl ever got away with breaking a single law there. That was because Chief of Police Brown's most difficult cases were solved by his son at the dinner table . . .

ENCYCLOPEDIA BROWN
Boy Detective

"IS THERE A DETECTIVE IN THE HOUSE? Then let him match wits with Encyclopedia Brown, the ten-year-old detective . . . Mr. Sobol's book is as bright and entertaining as its hero."
—*The New York Times*

ENCYCLOPEDIA BROWN
Boy Detective

BY DONALD J. SOBOL

Illustrated by
Leonard Shortall

A BANTAM SKYLARK BOOK®
TORONTO · NEW YORK · LONDON · SYDNEY · AUCKLAND

*This low-priced Bantam Book
has been completely reset in a type face
designed for easy reading, and was printed
from new plates. It contains the complete
text of the original hard-cover edition.*
NOT ONE WORD HAS BEEN OMITTED.

RL 3, 008-012

ENCYCLOPEDIA BROWN BOY DETECTIVE

*A Bantam Book / published by arrangement with
Thomas Nelson Inc., Publishers*

PRINTING HISTORY

*Thomas Nelson edition published October 1963
15 printings through 1977*

Bantam Skylark edition / February 1978

2nd printing . . . . June 1978	7th printing . . . . . . May 1980
3rd printing . . November 1978	8th printing . . . . . . June 1980
4th printing . . . . May 1979	9th printing . September 1980
5th printing . . . . June 1979	10th printing . . . . . . June 1981
6th printing . . . November 1979	11th printing . . February 1982
12th printing . September 1982	

ISBN 0-553-15182-7

Published simultaneously in the United States and Canada

---

*Bantam Books are published by Bantam Books, Inc. Its trade-
mark, consisting of the words "Bantam Books" and the por-
trayal of a rooster, is Registered in U.S. Patent and Trademark
Office and in other countries. Marca Registrada. Bantam
Books, Inc., 666 Fifth Avenue, New York, New York 10103.*

PRINTED IN THE UNITED STATES OF AMERICA

C   21   20   19   18   17   16

For Ben and Julie Sobol

Contents

Encyclopedia Brown
Boy Detective

The Case of Natty Nat

Mr. and Mrs. Brown had one child. They called him Leroy, and so did his teachers.

Everyone else in Idaville called him Encyclopedia.

An encyclopedia is a book or a set of books giving information, arranged alphabetically, on all branches of knowledge.

Leroy Brown's head was like an encyclopedia. It was filled with facts he had learned from books. He was like a complete library walking around in sneakers.

Old ladies who did crossword puzzles

were always stopping him on the street to ask him questions.

Just last Sunday, after church, Mrs. Conway, the butcher's wife, had asked him: "What is a three-letter word for a Swiss river beginning with A?"

"Aar," Encyclopedia answered after a moment.

He always waited a moment. He wanted to be helpful. But he was afraid that people might not like him if he answered their questions too quickly and sounded *too* smart.

His father asked him more questions than anyone else. Mr. Brown was the chief of police of Idaville.

The town had four banks, three movie theaters, and a Little League. It had the usual number of gasoline stations, churches, schools, stores, and comfortable houses on shady streets. It even had a mansion or two, and some dingy sections. And it had the average number of crimes for a community of its size.

Idaville, however, only *looked* like the usual American town. It was, really, most *un*usual.

For nearly a whole year no criminal had

escaped arrest and no boy or girl had got away with breaking a single law in Idaville.

This was partly because the town's policemen were clever and brave. But mostly it was because Chief Brown was Encyclopedia's father.

His hardest cases were solved by Encyclopedia during dinner in the Browns' red brick house on Rover Avenue.

Everyone in the state thought that Idaville had about the smartest policemen in the world.

Of course, nobody knew a boy was the mastermind behind the town's police force.

You wouldn't guess it by looking at Encyclopedia. He looked like almost any fifth-grade boy and acted like one, too— except that he never talked about himself.

Mr. Brown never said a word about the advice his son gave him. Who would believe that his best detective was only ten years old?

This is how it began:

One evening at dinner, Mr. Brown said, "Natty Nat has struck again. He has held up another store—and right here in Idaville."

"What store, Dad?" asked Encyclopedia.

"The Men's Shop, owned by Mr. Dillon and Mr. Jones," answered Mr. Brown. "That makes six stores Natty Nat has held up in the state this month."

"Are you sure the robber was Natty Nat?" asked Encyclopedia.

"Mr. Dillon himself said it was Natty Nat," replied Mr. Brown.

He pulled a notebook from his pocket and put it beside his plate. "I wrote down everything Mr. Dillon told me about the holdup. I'll read it to you."

Encyclopedia closed his eyes. He always closed his eyes when he was getting ready to think hard.

His father began to read what Mr. Dillon, the storekeeper, had told him about the holdup:

I was alone in the store. I did not know anyone had come in. Suddenly a man's voice told me to raise my hands. I looked up then. I was face to face with the man the newspapers call Natty Nat. He had on a gray coat with a belt in the back, just as the newspapers said. He told me to turn and face the wall. Since he had a gun, I did as he said. When I turned around again, he was gone—with all the money.

Chief Brown finished reading and closed his notebook.

Encyclopedia asked only one question: "Did the newspapers ever print a picture of Natty Nat?"

"No," answered his father. "He never stands still long enough for a picture to be taken. Remember, he's never been caught. But every policeman in the state knows he always wears that gray coat with the belt in the back."

"Nobody even knows his real name," said Encyclopedia, half to himself. "Natty Nat is just what the newspapers call him."

Suddenly he opened his eyes. "Say, the only reason Mr. Dillon thought it was Natty Nat was because of that gray coat!" he said. "The case is solved!"

"There is nothing to solve," objected Chief Brown. "There is no mystery. Mr. Dillon was robbed. The holdup man was the same one who has been robbing other stores in the state."

"Not quite," said Encyclopedia. "There was no holdup at The Men's Shop."

"What do you mean?" exclaimed Mr. Brown.

"I mean Mr. Dillon wasn't robbed, Dad. He lied from beginning to end," answered Encyclopedia.

"Why should Mr. Dillon lie?" demanded his father.

"I guess he spent the money. He didn't want his partner, Mr. Jones, to know it was missing," said Encyclopedia. "So Mr. Dillon said he was robbed."

"Leroy," said his mother, "please explain what you are saying."

"It's simple, Mom," said Encyclopedia. "Mr. Dillon read all about Natty Nat in the newspapers. So he knew Natty Nat always wore a gray coat with a belt in the back when he held up stores."

"Go on, Leroy," said Mr. Brown, leaning forward.

"Mr. Dillon knew it would sound much better if he could blame his holdup on someone people have read about," said Encyclopedia. "He said he knew it was Natty Nat because of the coat he wore—"

"That could be true," Chief Brown said.

"That *couldn't* be true," said Encyclope-

"Go on, Leroy," said Mr. Brown.

dia. "Mr. Dillon never saw the back of the man who held him up. He said so himself. Remember?"

Chief Brown frowned. He picked up his notebook again. He read to himself a while.

Then he fairly shouted, "Leroy, I believe you are right!"

Encyclopedia said, "Mr. Dillon only saw the *front* of the holdup man. He had no way of knowing that the man's coat had a belt *in the back*!"

"He stole money from his own store and from his partner too," cried Chief Brown. "And he nearly got away with it!"

He rushed from the dining room.

"Leroy," said Mrs. Brown, "did you get this idea from a television program?"

"No," said Encyclopedia. "I got it from a book I read about a great detective and his methods of observation."

"Well," said his mother proudly, "this proves how important it is to listen carefully and watch closely, to train your memory. Perhaps *you* will be a detective when you grow up."

"Mom," said Encyclopedia, "can I have another piece of pie?"

Mrs. Brown sighed. She had taught English in the Idaville High School before her marriage. "You *may* have another piece of pie," she said.

The Case of the Scattered Cards

At nine o'clock that night Encyclopedia climbed into bed. He lay awake a long time. He thought over what his mother had said to him about being a detective when he grew up.

In the morning he made up his mind.

He would go into the detective business and help people. He wouldn't wait until he grew up. It was summer and school was out. He could begin at once.

Encyclopedia got out of bed and searched through his closet. He dug out a toy printing press, a Christmas gift from his Uncle Ben two years ago.

As soon as Encyclopedia finished breakfast, he printed fifty handbills. When the ink was dry, he put the handbills in all the mailboxes in the neighborhood.

Then he went home and asked his mother for a big piece of cardboard. She gave him a dress box from the Bon Ton Store, which she had been saving. Encyclopedia borrowed the kitchen shears and cut out a square piece of cardboard. He took a black crayon and carefully lettered a sign.

The handbills and the sign said:

BROWN DETECTIVE AGENCY
13 Rover Avenue
Leroy Brown, President
No case too small
25¢ per day
plus expenses

Encyclopedia nailed the sign on the door of the Browns' garage.

The next morning he sat in the garage, waiting for somebody with a problem to drop in. Nobody dropped in. Only the rain. The roof of the garage had a hole in it.

Rain fell all morning, all afternoon, and all the next day.

Encyclopedia stared at the rain and felt lower than a submarine's bottom. He thought about taking down the sign and going to see what new teeth Charlie Stewart had added to his collection. Or maybe digging for worms with Billy and Jody Turner and fishing off the bridge at Mill Creek.

Suddenly a pair of rubbers and a raincoat appeared in the doorway. Inside them was a small boy.

"My name is Clarence Smith," said the boy. "I need your help."

"No case is too small," said Encyclopedia. "Is it murder?"

"No—" said Clarence, backing away.

"Kidnapping?" asked Encyclopedia. "Blackmail?"

"No—no," said Clarence weakly. "It's a tent."

He placed a quarter on the gasoline can beside Encyclopedia. "The tent is mine. But the Tigers say it's theirs."

"You are having trouble with talking tigers?" Encyclopedia asked.

"Oh, no," replied Clarence. "Tigers—that's the name of a boys' club near the canal. The boys are plenty tough, all of them. But their leader, Bugs Meany, is the toughest one."

"Take me to their leader," commanded Encyclopedia, "and to your tent."

"I'll do both," said Clarence. "Bugs Meany is sitting in the tent this very minute."

After a short walk, the two boys came to the tent. It stood in the woods between the canal and the Pierce Junk Yard.

Six older boys were sitting around a wooden box inside the tent. They were playing cards.

"Which one of you is Bugs Meany?" asked Encyclopedia.

"Me," said the biggest and dirtiest boy. "What's it to you?"

"You are in *my* tent," squeaked Clarence. "I found it. I mended all the holes in it."

"Scram!" growled Bugs.

"You know I found the tent in the junk

"Which one of you is Bugs Meany?"

yard," said Clarence. "You watched me put it up here last week."

"Get going," said Bugs. "I saw you steal it from our clubhouse this morning."

"Mind if I come in out of the rain?" Encyclopedia asked. As he ducked inside the tent, one of his feet hit an extra pack of cards lying beside the wooden box. The cards were scattered over the ground.

"Hey! What's the big idea?" said Bugs.

"The idea is a simple one," said the private detective. "See these cards? They are dry and not the least bit muddy, though I scattered them over the ground. Clarence didn't steal this tent from your clubhouse."

Bugs closed his hands into fists. His chin sprang out like the drawer of a cash register. "Are you calling *me* a liar?"

"Of course not," said Encyclopedia. "I'm simply going to tell you what I'll tell the police."

Encyclopedia spoke quietly into the older boy's right ear. Bugs listened. His face grew red, and then redder.

Suddenly he called, "Come on, Tigers! Let's get back to the clubhouse. It's no fun here."

When the Tigers had left, Clarence said to Encyclopedia, "Gosh, what did you say to Bugs?"

Encyclopedia smiled. "I pointed out why you couldn't have stolen the tent from the Tigers' clubhouse."

HOW DID ENCYCLOPEDIA KNOW?

*(Turn to page 103 for the solution to
The Case of the Scattered Cards.)*

The Case of the Civil War Sword

A boy with red hair stopped in the door-way of the Brown Detective Agency.

"Are you any good at swords?" he asked.

Encyclopedia did not lift his eyes from his book, *How to Build a Nuclear Reactor*.

"What kind of a game is swords?" he asked.

"It isn't a game," said the red-haired boy. "My name is Peter Clinton. I want to hire you."

Peter put two dimes and a nickel on the gasoline can beside Encyclopedia.

The coins clinked. Encyclopedia

stopped reading. He looked up, very businesslike.

"How can I help you?" he asked.

"I have a chance to trade my bicycle for a sword," said Peter. "I want to make sure the sword is real."

"You don't think the sword is really a sword?" said Encyclopedia. "What do you think it is?"

"That isn't what I mean," Peter said. "It's a sword from the Civil War—"

"There are thousands of swords left over from the Civil War," said Encyclopedia.

"I know," said Peter. "But how many belonged to General Jackson?"

"*Stonewall* Jackson?" gasped Encyclopedia. "The great Southern general?"

"This sword is supposed to have belonged to Stonewall Jackson," said Peter. "Bugs Meany says so."

"Bugs?" Encyclopedia straightened up at the name. "You want me to make sure the sword really did belong to Stonewall Jackson?"

"Yes," said Peter. "Then you'll take the case?"

"I'll take it," said Encyclopedia. "If Bugs is behind the trade, you'll need help."

Peter led the private detective to the Tigers' clubhouse, an unused tool shed behind Mr. Sweeney's Auto Body Shop. The Tigers were busy racing garter snakes.

Bugs made a face when he saw Encyclopedia.

"So Mr. Brains is now a Civil War know-it-all," said the Tigers' leader. "Well, well! Maybe you can tell me what Stonewall Jackson did at the Battle of Bull Run."

"Which battle at Bull Run?" asked Encyclopedia. "There were two—one in 1861, the other in 1862."

"Good for you," said Bugs, grinning. "Now don't say this sword isn't the real thing."

Encyclopedia walked to the table on which the sword lay.

Bugs said, "This sword was given to Stonewall Jackson a month after the First Battle of Bull Run."

"If that's true," Peter whispered to Encyclopedia, "the sword is worth ten bikes like mine."

"Twenty," corrected Encyclopedia.

"Read what it says on the blade," said Bugs.

Encyclopedia read:

27

"The sword is worth ten bikes like mine."

To Thomas J. Jackson, for standing like a stone wall at the First Battle of Bull Run on July 21, 1861. This sword is presented to him by his men on August 21, 1861.

"The sword certainly has seen a lot of use," said Encyclopedia.

"Did you expect it to look new and shiny?" sneered Bugs. "It's more than a hundred years old."

"It doesn't look like it ever was worth five dollars," Encyclopedia said.

"Never mind how it *looks*," said Peter. "Do you think it belonged to General Jackson?"

Before Encyclopedia could answer, Bugs spoke up. "I sure hate to part with the sword," he said. "But Peter wants it so much I just had to say I'd trade it for his bike."

"Trade? You won't trade with Peter," said Encyclopedia. "This sword never belonged to General Stonewall Jackson!"

HOW DID ENCYCLOPEDIA KNOW?

(Turn to page 104 for the solution to The Case of the Civil War Sword.)

The Case of Merko's Grandson

Bugs Meany and his Tigers liked to spend rainy afternoons in their clubhouse. Usually, they sat around thinking up ways of getting even with Encyclopedia Brown.

But today they had met for another purpose—to cheer the boy detective on.

Encyclopedia and Sally Kimball were about to meet in a battle of brains.

The Tigers hated Sally even more than they hated Encyclopedia—and with good reason.

When Sally had moved into the neighborhood two months ago, the Tigers jumped to show off for her. She was very pretty and she was very good at sports.

In fact, she got up a team of fifth-grade girls and challenged the Tigers to a game of softball. The boys thought it was a big joke, till Sally started striking them out. She was the whole team. In the last inning she hit the home run that won for the girls, 1–0.

But the real blow fell on the Tigers the next day.

Bugs was bullying a small boy when Sally happened to ride by on her bicycle.

"Let him go!" she ordered, hopping to the ground.

Bugs snarled. The snarl changed to a gasp as Sally broke his grip on the boy.

Before the other Tigers knew what to do, Sally had knocked their leader down with a quick left to the jaw.

Bugs bounced up, surprised and angry. He pushed Sally. She hit him again, with a right to the jaw. Bugs said *oooh,* and went down again.

For the next thirty seconds Bugs bounced up and down like a beach ball. By the fourth bounce, he was getting up a lot more slowly than he was going down.

"I'm going to make you sorry," he said.

But his voice was weak, and he wore the sick smile of a boy who had taken one ride too many on a roller coaster.

"So?" said Sally. She moved her feet and took careful aim.

"This," she said, aiming another blow, "should take the frosting off you."

Bugs landed on his back, flat as a fifteen-cent sandwich. Not until Sally had ridden away did he dare get up.

Sally was not content to rest on her victories at softball and fighting. She aimed higher.

She set out to prove she was not only stronger than any boy up to twelve years of age in Idaville, but smarter, too!

That meant out-thinking the thinking machine, Encyclopedia Brown.

The great battle of brains took place in the Tigers' clubhouse. The two champions, seated on orange crates, faced each other. The Tigers crowded behind Encyclopedia. The girls' softball team crowded behind Sally. That left just enough room in the tool shed to think.

Everyone stopped talking when Peter Clinton, the referee, announced the rules.

"Sally has five minutes to tell a mystery.

The two champions faced each other.

She must give all the clues. Then Encyclopedia will have five minutes to solve the mystery. Ready, you two?"

"Ready," said the girl champion.

"Ready," said Encyclopedia, closing his eyes.

"Go!" called Peter, eyes on his watch.

Sally began to tell the story:

"The Great Merko was the best trapeze artist the world had ever seen. People in every big city were thrilled by the wonderful performer swinging fifty feet above the ground!

"In the year 1922, Merko died at the very height of fame. In Merko's desk was found a letter. It was a will, written by the circus star. The will directed that the star's money be put in a bank for forty years.

"After forty years, the money was to be taken out and given to Merko's oldest grandson. If no grandson was alive, all the money was to go to Merko's nearest relative, man or woman.

"Forty years passed. A search was begun. At last a man was found in Kansas City who said he was Merko's grandson. His name was Fred Gibson. He went to court to claim his inheritance.

"While the judge was listening to him, a tall woman in the back of the courtroom jumped up. She was very excited.

"The woman said she was the trapeze artist's grandniece. She kept shouting that the Great Merko was not Fred Gibson's grandfather. Therefore, the money was rightfully hers.

"The judge questioned the woman. He had to agree with what she said. She was Merko's grandniece, and the Great Merko was *not* Fred Gibson's grandfather.

"Now," concluded Sally. "Who got Merko's money—the tall woman or Fred Gibson?"

Sally wore a smile of triumph as she looked at Encyclopedia.

The tool shed was still. The boys looked at their shoes. Had Sally beaten them again? Had Encyclopedia met his master?

Encyclopedia had five short minutes to solve the brain-twister.

Slowly the minutes ticked away. One . . . two . . . three . . . four . . .

Encyclopedia stirred on his orange crate. He opened his eyes. He smiled at Sally.

"You told it very cleverly," he said. "I nearly said the wrong person. But the answer is really quite simple."

Encyclopedia rose to leave. "The Great Merko's money went to Fred Gibson."

WHY?

(Turn to page 105 for the solution to The Case of Merko's Grandson.)

The Case of the Bank Robber

"Three dollars and fifty cents!" exclaimed Encyclopedia, as he finished counting the money in the treasury of the Brown Detective Agency. "Business is booming."

"You should put that money in a bank," said Sally Kimball, whom Encyclopedia had made his bodyguard and junior partner. "Money isn't safe in a shoe box."

"Maybe you're right," said Encyclopedia. "Sometimes even shoes aren't safe in a shoe box. It would look awful if a detective agency was robbed!"

The partners talked it over. They de-

cided to take the money downtown to a
bank and start a savings account.

It was too far to ride on their bicycles, so
they took the bus. They got off near the
Corning National Bank on Beech Street.
As they stepped out of the bus, they heard
the sound of shooting.

At first Encyclopedia thought the bus
had backfired. A moment later he saw a
man in the doorway of the bank.

The man wore a hat. A handkerchief
covered the lower part of his face. In one
hand he held a yellow paper bag. With the
other he waved a gun.

Somebody shouted, "Holdup! Holdup!"
Then, all at once, everybody was running,
trying to get out of the robber's way.

The man with the gun turned and fled. In
his haste he did not seem to look where he
was going. He ran into a beggar wearing
dark glasses and carrying a white cane and
tin cup.

The beggar's cane and cup flew into the
street. The robber and the beggar fell to the
sidewalk. They rolled about together for a
few seconds before the robber broke away
and got to his feet.

He raced down the street just as a police

car drew up before the bank. Chief Brown and one of his officers leaped out of the car and ran after the robber.

"We caught him," said Chief Brown at dinner that night. "He led us a merry chase, but we got him. The trouble is we can't charge him with the robbery."

"But why not?" Mrs. Brown demanded.

"Yes, Dad, why not?" Encyclopedia asked. "Wasn't the money he stole in that yellow paper bag he was carrying?"

Chief Brown laid down his fork. "Do you know what we found in that yellow bag of his? Money? No. A loaf of white bread! He resisted police officers, but I don't know how long we can keep him in jail."

"Are you sure you caught the right man, Dad?" Encyclopedia said.

"We'll have a hard time proving it," said Chief Brown. "No one can identify him. And nobody saw the robber's face. He wore a handkerchief over his nose and mouth and his hat was pulled down over his forehead and eyes. This man we picked up is wearing a brown suit, and the teller at the bank says the robber wore a suit the same color. And, of course, there is the yellow bag. But where's the money?"

"Does the man you picked up have any distinguishing features?" Encyclopedia wanted to know.

"Well, he has a pug nose and a scar running down one cheek. But remember, no one saw the robber's face," said Chief Brown. "I can hold him in jail overnight for resisting a police officer. That's about all."

"I never saw a beggar in Idaville before today," said Encyclopedia thoughtfully.

"Oh, the blind man," said Chief Brown. "He seems like a nice old fellow. He calls himself 'Blind Tom.' I hated to tell him it's against the law to beg here."

"The poor man," said Mrs. Brown. "Won't the Salvation Army help him?"

"Yes," replied Chief Brown. "But he said he likes being on his own. He promised to leave town tomorrow."

"Where is he staying?" asked Encyclopedia.

"At the old Martin Inn," answered Chief Brown. "One of those buildings in the row down by the railroad tracks. Why do you ask? Have you got an idea about this case, Leroy?"

"No," mumbled Encyclopedia.

Mrs. Brown looked hurt. She had come

to expect her son to solve a case before dessert.

After dinner, Encyclopedia walked over to Sally's house. "I have to work this evening," he said. "I may need you. Want to come?"

"Oh, boy, do I!" Sally sang out.

The sky was growing dark as the two detectives rode their bicycles down a dingy block west of the railroad station.

"Who lives *here*?" asked Sally as Encyclopedia stopped in front of a run-down hotel.

"Blind Tom, the beggar. He'll be leaving town tomorrow. That's why we have to see him this evening."

"Do you think he can help us?" asked Sally.

"I think so. A blind man sees with his hands," replied Encyclopedia. "Remember how the beggar rolled with the robber on the sidewalk? If he *felt* the robber's face through the handkerchief, he might know him again."

"I get it," said Sally. "If he could feel the man's face again, he might know whether the man your father caught is really the robber!"

"Who lives here?" Sally asked.

"Right," answered Encyclopedia.

"Gosh," said Sally, "I hope he hasn't left town yet!"

Inside the hotel, the desk clerk gave the two young detectives some help. Blind Tom lived alone. His room was Number 214.

Sally and Encyclopedia climbed the dark, creaky stairs to the second floor. They knocked on the door numbered 214. Nobody answered.

"Look, the door's not shut," whispered Sally. "Shall I—"

Encyclopedia nodded.

Sally pushed the door till it swung open so that they could look into the room.

The room was small and shabby. Against the far wall stood an iron bed. A small reading lamp cast its light upon a copy of the *Idaville Daily News* that lay open on the pillow.

Suddenly the tapping of a cane sounded in the hall. Tap . . . tap . . . tap . . .

Blind Tom came up behind Sally.

"Is someone here?" he asked. "I haven't had a visitor in a long time. I wasn't expecting anyone tonight, but it's nice to have you." He lifted his cane. "Won't you come in?"

"No thanks!" said Encyclopedia. He pushed Sally down the hall and hurried her down the stairs.

She didn't have a chance to catch her breath until they were outside the hotel.

"Why the big rush?" Sally asked. "I thought you were going to ask Blind Tom if he could recognize the man who robbed the bank this afternoon."

"I don't have to ask him," replied Encyclopedia. "Blind Tom knows the robber, because Blind Tom helped in the robbery!"

HOW DID ENCYCLOPEDIA KNOW?

(Turn to page 106 for the solution to The Case of the Bank Robber.)

The Case of the Happy Nephew

The Browns were having left-over meat loaf for dinner one night when the telephone rang.

"It must be important," said Mrs. Brown worriedly. "Otherwise why would anyone call during the dinner hour?"

She hurried to the telephone. In a moment she called to her husband, "It's Officer Carlson, dear."

Chief Brown went to the telephone and spoke with his officer for several minutes. When he returned to the dining room, he wore a frown—and his gun.

"The Princess Bake Shop on Vine Street

was robbed less than an hour ago," he said. "I'll have to go out."

"Any clues, Dad?" asked Encyclopedia.

"We have an eyewitness," answered his father. "A man passing the bakery says he saw John Abbot running out the door."

"Hasn't John Abbot been in prison?" asked Mrs. Brown.

"Five years ago," said Chief Brown. "But he's gone straight ever since he came out. The eyewitness only got a quick look at the robber; he might be mistaken."

Chief Brown shrugged. "Still, I suppose I'll have to stop by and question John. I hope he has a good alibi."

"Can I go with you?" cried Encyclopedia.

"*May* I go with you," his mother said. "And drink your milk first."

"*May* I go with you, Dad?" Encyclopedia asked. He gulped his milk.

"Come along if you like," said his father. "But you will have to stay in the car—and be quiet."

"I'll be as quiet as a cat at a dog show," promised Encyclopedia.

He sat quietly beside his father in the police car on the drive to the house where

John Abbot lived with his sister and her family.

"Staying in the car won't be so bad," Encyclopedia decided. "The car will be a lot closer to the case than our dining room."

On the west side of town his father stopped the car. "Here's the house."

Encyclopedia saw a small white house in need of paint. An old yellow car stood in the shaded driveway.

"There's John," said Chief Brown.

A tall young man had come out of the house. He was carrying a barefoot boy about a year and a half old.

Chief Brown reminded Encyclopedia to sit quietly in the car. Then he got out and walked toward John Abbot.

"Put the child down, John," Chief Brown called. "And keep your hands where I can see them."

John Abbot started to lower the barefoot baby onto the sharp stones of the gravel driveway. Then he changed his mind and put the child on the front fender of the yellow car, and raised his hands.

"What's this all about, Chief?" he asked.

"Robbery," replied Chief Brown. "You were seen running out of the Princess

Bake Shop on Vine Street an hour ago. The door was broken and all the money in the cash register was stolen."

John Abbot laughed. "I wasn't near Vine Street an hour ago. Why, all day—"

"Look out!" shouted Chief Brown. He leaped for the baby.

The child had climbed onto the hood of the yellow car. He smiled and gurgled happily. Suddenly he stood up and walked close to the edge of the hood. Chief Brown caught him just as he started to fall off the car.

"Thanks, Chief," said John Abbot. "He's my nephew. I'll hold him."

"No, I'll hold him," said Chief Brown. "Just tell me where you were today."

"Anyone who says he saw me coming out of the Princess Bake Shop an hour ago is either crazy or a liar," said John Abbot.

"Can you prove you were somewhere else?"

"I was miles away," said John Abbot. "Since eight o'clock this morning I've been driving this car. I drove down from Sundale Shores. I got here just five minutes before you came."

Chief Brown looked at his watch. "You

"*Look out!*" *shouted Chief Brown.*

drove six hundred miles in less than twelve hours," he said. "Did you stop around six o'clock and talk to anyone? Somebody we can check your story with?"

"No, not around six o'clock," said John Abbot. "I stopped for gas and a hamburger about four-thirty. Then I drove straight through. I didn't break any speed limit. And I had nothing to do with any bake shop robbery!"

"I'd like to think you are telling the truth," said Chief Brown.

"I am. I've gone straight, believe me," said John Abbot.

"All right," said Chief Brown. "I'll have to question the eyewitness who says he saw you. Maybe it will turn out that he isn't sure."

Chief Brown put the baby in John Abbot's arms and walked back to the police car.

"I heard and saw everything, Dad," said Encyclopedia. "How come you didn't arrest him?"

"Because he says he was driving from Sundale Shores when the robbery took place," answered Chief Brown. "He got here just five minutes before we came. I can't prove he is lying. At least not yet."

He slipped into the seat beside Encyclopedia, and started the car.

"Listen to me, Leroy," he said. "Our eyewitness may have made a mistake. He may have seen a man who only looked like John Abbot. A good police officer doesn't put people in jail without more proof than that."

"I believe the witness," said Encyclopedia. "John Abbot didn't just drive in from Sundale Shores in that old yellow car. I can prove he didn't!"

WHAT WAS THE PROOF?

(Turn to page 107 for the solution to The Case of the Happy Nephew.)

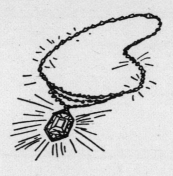

The Case of
the Diamond Necklace

"You've hardly touched your soup," said Mrs. Brown. "Something is wrong."

"I'm not hungry," said Chief Brown. He pushed his chair back from the dining table.

"It's that Van Tweedle case," said Mrs. Brown. "Now stop blaming yourself."

"What happened, Dad?" asked Encyclopedia.

"I wish I knew," answered his father. "Last night I was at Mrs. Van Tweedle's yearly party for the Community Chest

Drive. I was guarding a diamond necklace."

He drew a deep breath. "The necklace was stolen right under my nose!"

"Mrs. Van Tweedle must have been afraid it might be stolen," said Encyclopedia. "Was that why she asked you to guard it?"

Chief Brown nodded. "She received an unsigned letter last week. It told her to put ten thousand dollars in cash behind the statue of George Washington in the park. If she refused to do this, her necklace would be stolen."

"Wow!" exclaimed Encyclopedia. "Is the necklace really worth ten thousand dollars?"

"More," said his father. "Want the facts?"

Encyclopedia closed his eyes and prepared for some hard thinking. "Go ahead, Dad."

"Mrs. Van Tweedle planned to give the necklace away during the party," Chief Brown began. "That is, she was going to sell it to the highest bidder on the stroke of midnight. The money was to go to the Community Chest.

"To show off the necklace, Mrs. Van Tweedle's old college roommate, Miss Stark, wore it at the party. At first, I didn't let Miss Stark out of my sight.

"Around eleven o'clock Miss Stark said she felt ill. She went upstairs to the guest room. She said she wanted to rest a little while.

"I went into the room ahead of her. I wanted to make sure no one was there. Then I had her lock the door. And I stood guard in the hall.

"Ten minutes passed. Suddenly I heard her scream. A few seconds later, two shots rang out. I called to Miss Stark. She didn't answer.

"I broke down the locked door. Miss Stark was lying on the bed in a faint. The necklace was gone from her neck.

"When she came to, she could tell me little. Everything had happened so quickly. She had heard nothing. And she had fainted before she could see the thief, she said.

"The thief must have got in and out by the window. Two bullets were in the wall above the bed. Miss Stark was lucky that she wasn't killed!"

Encyclopedia's father finished speaking. A silence fell over the Browns' dining room.

Then Encyclopedia asked one question:

"Was Miss Stark left alone in the room after you broke in?"

Chief Brown looked surprised at this question. He thought a bit before answering.

"Let me see. . . . I was with her all the time. Mrs. Van Tweedle came up to the room as soon as she heard the racket. Then the doctor came. He took Miss Stark directly to the hospital. He never left her side."

"The hospital?" said Mrs. Brown. "The poor girl. She must have had a terrible scare!"

"She was pretty badly shaken," said Chief Brown. "The doctor ordered complete rest and quiet. She has to stay in the hospital until tomorrow."

"Good," said Encyclopedia, opening his eyes. "But there is no time to lose. Her room must be searched before she gets back."

"Searched for what?" asked Chief Brown.

"For the necklace," said Encyclopedia. "And the gun."

"Leroy!" exclaimed Mrs. Brown. "Do you think the thief would be so silly as to leave the necklace and the gun behind?"

"She did," said Encyclopedia calmly. "She had no choice."

"*She!*" gasped Chief Brown. "Do you mean Miss Stark? What makes you think she did it?"

"It's quite simple," said Encyclopedia. "First she tried to get ten thousand dollars out of her old classmate by writing that letter."

"But the letter didn't work," Chief Brown said. "Mrs. Van Tweedle hired me to guard the necklace. The letter only made it tougher for Miss Stark."

"She didn't think it would," Encyclopedia pointed out. "She must have talked Mrs. Van Tweedle into letting her wear the necklace at the party."

"The whole idea sounds pretty weak to me," said Chief Brown. "Think how fast Miss Stark would have had to work. She would have had to hide the necklace and the gun after she fired the two shots into the wall. She must have known I'd break down the door the instant I heard the gun go off in the room."

"She hid the necklace before she fired the shots," said Encyclopedia.

"Well, if you are right, the gun and the necklace are still in the room," said Chief Brown. "I'll telephone one of my men to search it right away."

An hour later Officer Murphy called back. Mrs. Van Tweedle's guest room had been searched. The necklace and the gun had been found, hidden in a hatbox on a closet shelf.

The Browns had finished dinner. Encyclopedia was in the kitchen drying dishes for his mother when he heard the news.

"Miss Stark expects to leave the hospital tomorrow a rich woman," said Encyclopedia.

"All she had to do, she thought, was to go back to the room and pick up the hatbox with the gun and necklace," said Chief Brown.

"She might have got away with it," said

He was drying dishes when he heard the news.

Encyclopedia. "But every crook makes one mistake!"

WHAT WAS MISS STARK'S MISTAKE?

(Turn to page 108 for the solution to The Case of the Diamond Necklace.)

The Case of
the Knife in the Watermelon

Mr. Patch was the first grown-up to come to the Brown Detective Agency. He was carrying a watermelon.

Mr. Patch owned a grocery store. He showed the watermelon to Encyclopedia. It had a knife buried in it up to the handle.

"Find the boy who owns this knife!" roared Mr. Patch. "Look what he did!"

Encyclopedia looked at the watermelon. "Stabbing a watermelon isn't against the law," he pointed out. "I mean, it's not the same as stabbing a person."

"The knife *ended* in my watermelon," Mr. Patch shouted. "It *started* in the window of my storeroom."

"Someone used the knife to break into your storeroom?"

"And to open my money box!" cried Mr. Patch.

"How much was stolen?" asked Encyclopedia.

"The thief didn't have time to take anything," said Mr. Patch, in a calmer voice. "He heard me coming and he got scared. When he started to run, he tripped and fell. His knife plunged into this watermelon. He didn't have time to pull it out."

"Did you see his face?"

Mr. Patch shook his head. "No, but I did see he had the letter **L** on the back of his jacket."

"That means he's a Lion—a member of the boys' club on Woodburn Avenue," said Encylopedia. "A real lead!"

The private detective stepped closer to the watermelon. The knife had plunged into it so deeply that only the carved wood handle showed above the green skin.

Mr. Patch laid a quarter on the gasoline can. "Find the owner of this knife, quick!"

"I'm sorry," replied Encyclopedia, thinking he would have to charge for expenses on this case. "I'll need a little time. I have to buy a fingerprint kit. Then I have to dust the handle of the knife and—"

"There are no fingerprints," said Mr. Patch heavily. "I wiped them off."

"Y-you wiped them off?" said Encyclopedia weakly.

Mr. Patch explained. "My cat knocked a bag of flour off a shelf. It broke and spilled over the watermelon and knife. I wiped off the flour—"

"And the fingerprints too!" Encyclopedia clasped his head and moaned. Then he looked up. "Still, the thief doesn't know that you wiped off his fingerprints—"

Encyclopedia took out his handkerchief. He wrapped it carefully around the handle of the knife.

"That does it," he said. "That makes it *look* as though we have fingerprints we are trying to save. The thief may try to wipe them off, and give himself away. We'll have to watch all the Lions. Let's go—"

Encyclopedia got into Mr. Patch's truck. They drove over to Woodburn Avenue. Four Lions—John, Frank, Corky, and

"There are no fingerprints," said Mr. Patch.

Buster—were outside the club, working on the engine of an old black car.

Although few in number, the Lions were all big boys—bigger than Bugs Meany. But Mr. Patch was bigger than any of them. He had strong hands and big arms. So the Lions listened when Encyclopedia spoke.

"Do you see this watermelon?" he asked. "Now I take off the handkerchief. There! What do you see?"

"The handle . . ." said Buster.

". . . of a knife," said Corky.

"Very interesting," said John.

"So what?" said Frank.

"The knife," said Encyclopedia, "was used in an attempt to rob Mr. Patch's store."

"The knife. . ." said Buster.

". . . doesn't belong . . ." said Corky.

". . . to any . . ." said John.

". . . of us," said Frank.

"Maybe not. But the police will probably take your fingerprints," said Encyclopedia. "If the guilty boy steps forward now, Mr. Patch will ask the police not to be too hard on him."

The Lions looked serious. Mr. Patch

looked serious. The only boy detective in the state looked serious.

But that was all.

"It's not working the way you planned," said Mr. Patch in a whisper. "None of them has tried to wipe the handle of the knife."

Encyclopedia nodded. "Leave the knife in the watermelon, just as it is. Don't touch it," he whispered back.

To the Lions he said, "The police will break up your club if they find one of you is a thief."

The Lions stopped looking serious. They looked scared.

Suddenly John said softly, "Frank owns a knife like that."

"A lot of fellows own knives with carved handles," retorted Frank. "Cut it out!"

"You showed me yours yesterday," John shot back. "You even tried to get me to hold it. Why, *my* fingerprints might be on that handle!"

"It's not the same knife," said Frank. "So quit worrying."

"I lost my knife last month," Buster said. "Everyone knows I did. Where is your knife, Corky?"

The Case of the Knife in the Watermelon

"I lost mine, too," said Corky. "This one couldn't be my knife, anyway. Mine has a blade a half inch longer."

None of the Lions remembered what the others' knives really looked like. They began to argue loudly. Each boy tried to put himself in the clear.

"Too bad," muttered Mr. Patch. "They are scared and fighting among themselves. But none of them has touched the knife to try to get rid of the fingerprints. Your plan didn't work."

"Yes, it did," said Encyclopedia. "I know whose knife it is."

HOW DID HE KNOW WHOSE KNIFE IT WAS?

*(Turn to page 109 for the solution to
The Case of the Knife in the Watermelon.)*

The Case of
the Missing Roller Skates

Between nine and nine-thirty on Tuesday morning Sally Kimball's roller skates disappeared from the waiting room in Dr. Vivian Wilson's office.

And where was Encyclopedia Brown, boy detective? He was not ten feet away from the scene of the crime. He was sitting in a chair, with his eyes shut and his mouth wide open!

In a way, he had an excuse.

Dr. Wilson was pulling one of Encyclopedia's teeth.

"There!" said Dr. Wilson. He said it

cheerfully, as if he were handing Encyclopedia an ice cream cone instead of a tooth.

"Ugh!" said Encyclopedia.

Dr. Wilson said, "All right. Hop down from the chair."

Encyclopedia hopped down and put the tooth in his pocket. He was going to give it to Charlie Stewart, who collected teeth and kept them in a flowered cookie jar.

Encyclopedia went into the waiting room. The chair on which he had left Sally's roller skates was empty!

He looked behind the chair. He dropped to his knees and looked under the chair.

"The skates—they're gone!" he exclaimed.

"Are you sure you brought them with you?" asked Dr. Wilson.

"I'm sure," answered Encyclopedia. "They were broken. I fixed them last night for my partner, Sally Kimball. I was going to take them over to her house on my way home from your office."

Dr. Wilson shook his head sadly. "I'm afraid you will never get them back."

But Dr. Wiison knew nothing about detective work. Encyclopedia liked the den-

"The skates—they're gone!"

tist, though he felt that Vivian was a better first name for a woman than a man.

"I'll find the skates," said the boy detective. He spoke with certainty. But he felt no such thing. What he felt was the blow to his pride; it hurt worse than his jaw.

Imagine a detective being robbed!

In the corridor outside Dr. Wilson's office, Encyclopedia leaned against the wall. He closed his eyes and did some deep thinking.

Dr. Wilson's office was on the ground floor of the new Medical Building. The building had three floors and fifteen offices. All the offices were used by doctors or dentists.

What if the thief had followed him into the building in order to steal the skates? Then the case was closed. "I could spend the rest of my life looking through closets, school lockers, and garages all over Idaville," Encyclopedia thought.

But suppose the thief had simply come into the building to see a doctor. Suppose, on his way in, he had noticed a boy carrying a pair of roller skates. Well, that was something else!

Encyclopedia reasoned further. "The

thief could be a grown-up, a boy, or a girl."

He ruled out a grown-up. First, because it was unlikely that a grown-up would steal an old pair of small skates. Second, because a grown-up would be too hard to catch. Too many men and women went in and out of the Medical Building every hour.

"I'll have to act on the idea that the thief is a boy or girl," he decided. "It's a long chance, but the only one I have."

He opened his eyes. The case called for plain, old-fashioned police leg work!

Encyclopedia began on the ground floor. He asked the same question in every office: "Were any boys or girls here to see the doctor this morning?"

The answer was the same in every office: "No."

Things looked hopeless. But on the top floor he finally got a lead. The nurse in room 301 told him a boy named Billy Haggerty had been there this morning to have a sprained wrist treated.

Encyclopedia asked in the last two offices, just to be sure. Neither doctor had treated children that morning.

Billy Haggerty became suspect number one!

Encyclopedia got Billy Haggerty's address from the nurse in room 301. He hurried back to Dr. Wilson's office to use the telephone. He called Sally. He told her to meet him in front of the Haggertys' house in half an hour.

"We may have some rough going ahead of us," he warned.

But Billy Haggerty turned out to be only an inch taller than Encyclopedia, and shorter than Sally.

Billy drew himself up to his full height at Encyclopedia's first question:

"Were you in Dr. Vivian Wilson's office this morning?"

"Naw," snapped Billy. "I don't know any Dr. Wilson."

"You didn't ask anyone about Dr. Wilson?" put in Sally.

"I never heard of him before you spoke his name," said Billy.

"Then you went straight to your own doctor on the third floor?" said Encyclopedia.

"Yeah. Dr. Stanton in room 301. What's it to you?"

"Dr. Wilson's office is down the hall from both the stairs and the elevator," said Encyclopedia thoughtfully. "You wouldn't pass his office going up or coming down."

"I don't know where his office is, and I don't care," said Billy. "It's none of your business where I was."

"We just want to be sure you weren't in Dr. Vivian Wilson's office this morning. That's all," said Sally.

"Well, I wasn't. I had a sprained wrist, not a toothache. So why should I go near his office?" demanded Billy. "I don't like snoopers. What are you after?"

"A pair of roller skates," said Encyclopedia. "Do you mind returning them? You've given yourself away."

WHAT GAVE BILLY AWAY?

(Turn to page 110 for the solution to The Case of the Missing Roller Skates.)

The Case of
the Champion Egg Spinner

Mr. O'Hara made the biggest and best chocolate ice cream sodas in Idaville. He used a double helping of ice cream in each and every one.

Encyclopedia went to Mr. O'Hara's drugstore on hot afternoons. When the detective business began to pay off, he went there on cool afternoons, too. But he never thought he would one day solve a case sitting at Mr. O'Hara's soda fountain.

People who sat at Mr. O'Hara's counter ordered a soft drink. Or ice cream. Sometimes they ordered both.

Nobody ever brought his *own* food.

But one Sunday a boy about twelve years old came into the drugstore carrying an egg. He put it on Mr. O'Hara's counter.

Encyclopedia was surprised. He had finished his soda, but he sat and watched the boy with the egg.

He was even more surprised when the boy spun the egg on the counter.

"Still practicing?" Mr. O'Hara asked the boy.

The boy smiled as if he owned the whole world. "Just keeping my touch. I've got a big match tomorrow."

He gave the egg another spin.

"He's good," thought Encyclopedia. "He really knows how to spin an egg to keep it going."

The boy ordered a chocolate soda with a triple helping of ice cream. That cost ten cents extra.

Mr. O'Hara made the soda. He placed it before the boy. He did not see the egg spinning toward the glass till it was too late.

The egg knocked against the glass and spun away. It dropped out of sight on Mr. O'Hara's side of the counter.

Mr. O'Hara looked down. "That's the end of your egg. I'm sorry."

"Forget it," said the boy with a grand wave of his hand. "I have to use another egg in the spinning match tomorrow anyway."

"I'd better sweep up the mess," said Mr. O'Hara. He walked to the back of the drugstore.

Encyclopedia left twenty-five cents on the counter to pay for his soda. As he went out the door, he saw Mr. O'Hara returning with a broom and a dustpan.

Encyclopedia rode home slowly on his bicycle. He stopped to look at the stuffed mountain lion Mr. Eckstrom, the taxidermist, had just put in the window of his shop. The boy detective was in no hurry. It was Sunday, and the Brown Detective Agency was closed.

As he turned the corner on Rover Avenue, he saw that something was up. Bicycles were parked on the lawn in front of his house. Just about the whole gang was waiting for him at the garage.

He made out Jody and Billy Turner, Charlie Stewart, Herb Stein, Pinky

Plummer, and Sally. They looked as happy as six flat tires.

Sally greeted him.

"The boys need your help," she said.

"With what?"

"With Eddie Phelan," said Charlie Stewart. "His egg beats everything."

"Who is this Eddie Phelan?" asked Encyclopedia. "A human egg beater?"

"Stop being silly," said Sally.

"Eddie is the champion egg spinner," explained Pinky. "He keeps his egg spinning longer than any one else's."

"The boys think he does something secret and unfair to win," said Sally.

"Ah, you fear foul play?" asked Encyclopedia.

"Be serious!" cried Sally. "Eddie won everything at the last match—Pinky's glove, Jody's bat, Charlie's hockey stick, Billy's magic set, and Herb's jackknife."

"There's another match tomorrow," said Jody. "Eddie is out to win Charlie's tooth collection."

"And I just got two zebra teeth," groaned Charlie. "Mr. Eckstrom gave them to me for delivering Dr. Webster's stuffed sail-fish Friday."

"Hmmm," said Encyclopedia. "I never heard of an egg spinning contest before. Who thought it up?"

"Eddie," said the five boys together.

"I might have known," said Encyclopedia.

"The boys have been practicing for days," said Sally. "But Eddie will walk off with Charlie's tooth collection just the same!"

"And everything else," said Billy.

"This case smells rotten," said Encyclopedia. "Where do you get the eggs?"

"At the supermarket," answered Pinky. "All of us go together."

"How do you know the egg Eddie got at the supermarket will be the one he uses tomorrow?"

"Each boy picks an egg," said Pinky. "He marks it with a pencil and gives his egg to another boy. That way we know no one can change an egg before the match."

"Who marked Eddie's egg?" asked Encyclopedia.

"I did," said Charlie. "I made a double X on it."

"Tomorrow you'll have to signal to me," said Encyclopedia, "before you start spinning. If the egg is the one you marked, raise one finger. If it isn't the one, raise two fingers. Got it?"

"Got it," said Charlie.

"Now where and when does the match take place?"

"Behind the school at nine in the morning," said Jody.

"I'll be there," said Encyclopedia, starting into the house.

The boys and Sally felt let down. They had expected Encyclopedia to solve this case right away.

"Oh, stop worrying," Encyclopedia called to them. "I have a pretty good idea why Eddie always wins."

The next morning when Encyclopedia reached the schoolyard, Sally rushed to meet him. She was breathless.

"I thought you wouldn't get here in time!" she said.

"I couldn't find one of my sneakers," the boy detective said, looking around him.

Sure enough! Eddie, the champion, was the boy he had seen in the drugstore.

"The case of the champion egg spinner is cracked," Encyclopedia said mysteriously.

Eddie was smiling as he fingered the flowered cookie jar that held Charlie's collection of teeth.

Against the teeth, Eddie was putting up a football uniform. It was a better prize than fifty-three teeth, Pinky's used science kit, Jody's rubber boots, Billy's fishing pole, or even Herb's old telescope.

"The match is going to start," Sally told Encyclopedia.

Charlie and Eddie got down on their knees. The spinning field was the smooth marble slab under the statue of Thomas Edison.

Each boy handed the other his egg. Eddie hardly glanced at Charlie's. But Charlie peered at the champion's egg a long time. He turned it over slowly. Then he held up one finger.

Eddie hadn't changed eggs. He was using the one Charlie had marked.

"Ready?" asked Eddie, smiling.

Charlie peered at the egg.

"*Do something—fast!*" Sally whispered to Encyclopedia.

"Get set—" Eddie called.

"Excuse me," said Encyclopedia. "Is this a contest of skill alone?"

"Huh?" said Eddie. "Why . . . of course."

"Then you won't mind changing eggs," said Encyclopedia. "Let Charlie have your egg, and you take his. The boy who spins his egg the longest wins the match."

Eddie's smile disappeared as fast as pancakes at Sunday breakfast. His hand closed quickly over his egg.

"Are you saying someone's cheating?" he demanded. "Not that it's any of your business, but Charlie knows this is my egg. It's the same one he marked."

"Of course, it's the same egg," said Encyclopedia. "But with one big difference that nobody can see!"

WHAT WAS THE DIFFERENCE?

*(Turn to page 111 for the solution to
The Case of the Champion Egg Spinner.)*

Bugs Meany said that Clarence had stolen the tent from the Tigers' clubhouse "this morning." That is, on the second day of the rain. Therefore, the ground under the tent should have been *wet*.

But when Encyclopedia scattered the cards with his foot, he discovered that the ground inside the tent was *dry*. This proved that the tent had been put up *before* the rain, as Clarence claimed—and not during the rain "this morning," as Bugs said.

Solution to *The Case of the Civil War Sword*

As soon as he had read the words on the blade, Encyclopedia knew the sword was a fake.

The two clues were the words *Bull Run* and *First*.

Jackson's men, being Southerners, would have called the battle by the South's name for it, the Battle of Manassas. Bull Run was the name given to the battle by the North.

Also, the sword was supposed to have been given to Stonewall Jackson in August 1861. No one could have known then that there would be another battle on the same spot the next year, in 1862.

Only after both battles had been fought would anyone have used the word *first* to describe the battle fought in 1861.

Solution to *The Case of Merko's Grandson*

Both the tall woman and Fred Gibson spoke the truth.

Although the Great Merko was not his grandfather, Fred Gibson was the Great Merko's grandson.

The Great Merko, as Encyclopedia realized, was a woman. She was Fred Gibson's *grandmother!*

Solution to *The Case of the Bank Robber*

Blind Tom was not expecting any visitors, he said. He also said that he had not had any visitors "in a long time." Yet the light in his room was on, and a newspaper lay on the pillow.

A blind man does not need a light, and he cannot read a newspaper. So Blind Tom was not blind at all.

Encyclopedia knew then why the beggar had not stepped out of the way of the bank robber. The two men had rolled on the sidewalk together with a purpose—to exchange yellow paper bags!

Blind Tom had slipped the robber the bag holding the loaf of bread, in order to fool the police if they caught him. The robber had slipped Blind Tom the bag holding the money.

Encyclopedia used a telephone in the store on the corner to call his father. Chief Brown hurried to the hotel. He found the money, still in the yellow paper bag, hidden under the mattress of Blind Tom's bed.

Blind Tom and the man the police were holding in jail confessed they had robbed the bank.

Solution to *The Case of the Happy Nephew*

John Abbot said he had reached his sister's house only "five minutes" before Chief Brown arrived. If John had just driven in from Sundale Shores, the motor and hood of his car would still have been burning hot. Remember, he said he had made only one stop—for a hamburger and gas—during the twelve-hour trip. If that was true, his little nephew, who was barefoot, would have cried out in pain when he stood on the hot hood of the car.

Instead, the baby smiled and gurgled happily. Therefore, the hood was *not* hot.

A cool hood meant that the car had not just been parked after a twelve-hour drive, as John Abbot said.

Miss Stark said that she did not see or hear the thief. Yet Chief Brown heard her scream, and "a few seconds later, two shots rang out."

Miss Stark's mistake was screaming *before* the shots were fired.

If she had not seen or heard anyone, she would have had no reason to be frightened. Only *after* the shots had been fired would she have screamed.

Solution to *The Case of the Knife in the Watermelon*

As Mr. Patch said, none of the Lions touched the knife. So the blade was buried in the watermelon all the time the Lions were looking at it.

In other words, none of the Lions could see how long the blade of the knife was.

But Corky said his knife had a blade that was "a half inch longer" than the one in the watermelon. That was his mistake.

He could not have known how long the blade was unless he had seen it before.

The knife belonged to Corky!

Billy Haggerty said that he had never heard of Dr. Vivian Wilson and that he didn't know where his office was. But he knew too much about him.

He knew that Dr. Vivian Wilson was (1) a man, not a woman, and (2) a dentist, not a doctor.

When he was tripped by his fibs, Billy returned the roller skates to Sally.

Mr. O'Hara had given Encyclopedia the clue to the mystery.

Remember how Eddie's egg had fallen off the counter onto the floor? What had Mr. O'Hara said? Not, "I'd better *clean up* the mess." No, he had said, "I'd better *sweep up* the mess."

He had not fetched a towel or mop; he had fetched a broom and a dustpan.

This told Encyclopedia the egg had broken into *pieces*. He realized that the egg was a hard-boiled one.

And a hard-boiled egg will spin longer than an uncooked egg, every time!

Eddie had to use another (uncooked!) egg against Charlie, and he lost the match. Charlie agreed to give back Eddie's football uniform if he would return the prizes he had won at the earlier matches.

The ex-champion returned the prizes.

ABOUT THE AUTHOR

DONALD J. SOBOL is the author of the highly acclaimed Encyclopedia Brown books. His awards for these books include the Pacific Northwest Reader's Choice Award for *Encyclopedia Brown Keeps the Peace* and a special Edgar from the Mystery Writers of America for his contribution to mystery writing in the United States.

Donald Sobol is married and has three children. A native of New York, he now lives in Florida.

Match Wits with America's
Sherlock Holmes in
Sneakers

ENCYCLOPEDIA BROWN

With a head full of facts and his eyes and ears on the world of Idaville, meet Leroy (Encyclopedia) Brown. Each Encyclopedia Brown book contains 10 baffling cases to challenge, stymie and amuse young sleuths. Best of all, the reader can try solving each case on his own before looking up the solution in the back of the book. "BRIGHT AND ENTERTAINING. . . ."
The New York Times
By Donald Sobol

☐ 15359	ENCYCLOPEDIA BROWN BOY DETECTIVE #1	$2.25
☐ 15392	ENCYCLOPEDIA BROWN/CASE OF THE SECRET PITCH #2	$2.25
☐ 15177	ENCYCLOPEDIA BROWN FINDS THE CLUE #3	$2.25
☐ 15411	ENCYCLOPEDIA BROWN GETS HIS MAN #4	$2.25
☐ 15404	ENCYCLOPEDIA BROWN KEEPS THE PEACE #6	$2.25
☐ 15389	ENCYCLOPEDIA BROWN SAVES THE DAY #7	$2.25
☐ 15410	ENCYCLOPEDIA BROWN TRACKS THEM DOWN #8	$2.25
☐ 15393	ENCYCLOPEDIA BROWN SHOWS THE WAY #9	$2.25
☐ 15423	ENCYCLOPEDIA BROWN TAKES THE CASE #10	$2.25
☐ 15371	ENCYCLOPEDIA BROWN & THE CASE OF THE MIDNIGHT VISITOR #13	$2.25
☐ 15352	ENCYCLOPEDIA BROWN AND THE MYSTERIOUS HANDPRINTS #16	$2.25

Prices and availability subject to change without notice.

Buy them at your local bookstore or use this handy coupon for ordering:

THE ENCYCLOPEDIA BROWN WACKY-BUT-TRUE SERIES!
written by Donald J. Sobol These stories are nutty, wacky . . .
and true! Meet Encyclopedia Brown, also known as Leroy, a
boy with a head full of facts and his eyes and ears on the
world of crime, mystery and intrigue. He's become a best
friend to many, and you'll join the ranks as you read these
funny, fact-filled books.

☐ **MISS KNOW IT ALL**   15292/$1.95
☐ **MISS KNOW IT ALL RETURNS**   15351/$2.25
  by Carol Beach York
  Miss Know It All appears suddenly one morning on the door-
  stop of the Good Day Home for Girls. All 28 girls are amazed
  at all Miss Know It All knows. But something happens to
  make the girls fear that they will lose their wonderful Miss
  Know It All forever! Both these warm and delightful books
  must reading.

☐ **DOWNTOWN FAIRY**   15170/$1.75
GODMOTHER
  by Charlotte Pomerantz
  "If only," wishes Olivia "I had a fairy godmother!" Suddenly
  out of a glimmer of blue light a plump woman with sparkling
  blue eyes appears. Olivia now has her fairy grandmother who
  immediately makes her invisible, and takes her on a fabulous
  adventure that changes Olivia's life forever.

☐ **HELP, THERE'S A CAT**   15199/$2.25
WASHING IN HERE
  by Alison Smith
  Henry Walker has a choice: he can keep house for his youn-
  ger brother and sister while his mother is busy or else horrible
  Aunt Wilhelmina will come to stay. Henry decides to take
  charge, but he wasn't prepared for Kitty, a 20-pound yellow-
  eyed monster cat.

☐ **JACOB TWO-TWO MEETS**   42075/$2.95
THE HOODED FANG
by Mordechai Richler
Jacob Two-Two says everything twice because no one listens to him the first time. But then he is convicted of insulting a grown-up and exiled to Slimer's Isle—a nightmarish prison guarded by wolverines and slithering snakes and the dreaded Hooded Fang!

☐ **OWLS IN THE FAMILY**   15350/$2.25
by Farley Mowat
This is the hilarious true tale of two Saskatchewan owls; Wol is a wonderful bird who terrorizes everyone, and Weeps is a comical bird afraid of almost everything, except a dog named Mutt. There are laughs galore as these two shake up a neighborhood, turn a house topsy-turvy and even outsmart Mutt!

☐ **ARTHUR THE KID**   15169/$2.25
by Alan Coren
When the bumbling Black Hand Gang, the gofiest outlaws in the Wild West, advertise for a boss, who do they get? Arthur the Kid, of course!

BANTAM
SHOP-AT-HOME
C·A·T·A·L·O·G

Shop at home
for quality childrens books
and save money, too.

Now you can order books for the whole family from Bantam's latest listing of hundreds of titles including many fine children's books. *And* this special offer gives you an opportunity to purchase a Bantam book for only 50¢. Here's how:

By ordering any five books at the regular price per order, you can also choose any other single book listed (up to $4.95 value) for just 50¢. Some restrictions do apply, so for further details send for Bantam's listing of titles today.